Bank Street

ABOUT THE BANK STREET READY-TO-READ SERIES

More than seventy-five years of educational research, innovative teaching, and quality publishing have earned The Bank Street College of Education its reputation as America's most trusted name in early childhood education.

Because no two children are exactly alike in their development, the Bank Street Ready-to-Read series is written on three levels to accommodate the individual stages of reading readiness of children ages three through eight.

○ *Level 1:* GETTING READY TO READ (Pre-K–Grade 1)
Level 1 books are perfect for reading aloud with children who are getting ready to read or just starting to read words or phrases. These books feature large type, repetition, and simple sentences.

○ *Level 2:* READING TOGETHER (Grades 1–3)
These books have slightly smaller type and longer sentences. They are ideal for children beginning to read by themselves who may need help.

● *Level 3:* I CAN READ IT MYSELF (Grades 2–3)
These stories are just right for children who can read independently. They offer more complex and challenging stories and sentences.

All three levels of The Bank Street Ready-to-Read books make it easy to select the books most appropriate for your child's development and enable him or her to grow with the series step by step. The levels purposely overlap to reinforce skills and further encourage reading.

We feel that making reading fun is the single most important thing anyone can do to help children become good readers. We hope you will become part of Bank Street's long tradition of learning through sharing.

The Bank Street
College of Education

For Bennett
— G.B.K.

For Jacob Harmon Lieberstein
— S.A.

For a free color catalog describing Gareth Stevens' list of high-quality books and multimedia programs, call 1-800-542-2595 (USA) or 1-800-461-9120 (Canada). Gareth Stevens Publishing's Fax: (414) 225-0377. See our catalog, too, on the World Wide Web: http://gsinc.com

Library of Congress Cataloging-in-Publication Data

Alexander, Sue.
    Who goes out on Halloween? / by Sue Alexander; illustrated by G. Brian Karas.
      p. cm. -- (Bank Street ready-to-read)
    Summary: Enumerates the various creatures out on Halloween, from fat monsters and pirates to small witches and ghosts.
    ISBN 0-8368-1759-1 (lib. bdg.)
    [1. Halloween--Fiction. 2. Stories in rhyme.] I. Karas, G. Brian, ill. II. Title. III. Series.
PZ8.3.A378Wh 1998
[E]--DC21
                                                    97-28945

This edition first published in 1998 by
Gareth Stevens Publishing
1555 North RiverCenter Drive, Suite 201
Milwaukee, Wisconsin 53212 USA

© 1990 by Byron Preiss Visual Publications, Inc. Text © 1990 by Sue Alexander.
Illustrations © 1990 by G. Brian Karas.

Published by arrangement with Bantam Doubleday Dell Books for Young Readers, a division of Bantam Doubleday Dell Publishing Group, Inc., New York, New York. All rights reserved.

Bank Street Ready To Read™ is a registered U.S. trademark of the Bank Street Group and Bantam Doubleday Dell Books For Young Readers, a division of Bantam Doubleday Dell Publishing Group, Inc.

Printed in Mexico

1 2 3 4 5 6 7 8 9 02 01 00 99 98

Bank Street Ready-to-Read™

Who Goes Out on Halloween?

by Sue Alexander
Illustrated by G. Brian Karas

A Byron Preiss Book

Gareth Stevens Publishing
MILWAUKEE

Who goes out on Halloween?

Who climbs up steps?
Who knocks on doors?

Tall witches.
Small witches.

6

Any-size- at-all witches.

Striped clowns.
Spotted clowns.

Even polka-dotted clowns.

Fat bunnies.
Skinny bunnies.

And some mini-bunnies.

11

Ghosts go out on Halloween.
Look! Here is one.

Who goes out on Halloween?

Tall pirates.
Small pirates.

Any-size-at-all pirates.

Striped cats.
Spotted cats.

Even polka-dotted cats.

Fat monsters.
Skinny monsters.

GRRRP

And some mini-monsters.

Space people go out
on Halloween.
See? Here they come!

Three by three,
and four by four!

Everyone goes out
on Halloween!

Witches and clowns walk
side by side.

Bunnies and ghosts look
for places to hide.

Pirates and cats
walk in a row.

Monsters and space people
see who they know.

They go by twos
and threes and fours.
They climb up steps.
They knock on doors.
They hold out bags.

30

And then they say . . .

31

Trick or Treat!